PRAISE FOR JA

The Guardian

Who wouldn't want to be swept off her feet by a movie star? And championed by a guardian angel? Sign me up! And like any great start to a series, the ending left me reaching for the next book. Highly recommended

— CHRISTINE HART

I was lucky to receive an advanced copy of The Guardian. A quick, easy read that I enjoyed!. A serious topic handled not only with touching moments but a few humorous moments also. Romance, suspense, family ties, friendship, angels that aren't sure about being angels, some sad moments, some nail biter moments, and a darling dog named Sugar Bear....what more could we want? I'm looking forward to the next book in this series.

— BARBARA CASSATA

The Sheriff Meets His Match

Who could possibly be the perfect match for Sheriff Jack Garrett, the steadfast pillar of a small west coast town like Tidal Falls? Enter Laurel Thomas, a woman on the run from her past in Florida. As soon as she shows up in Tidal Falls, she turns Jack's meticulously organized world upside down with her disorganized ways, sexy looks and feisty humor. I'd been craving Jack's story every since I read about him in an earlier story in the Wounded Hearts series, and I wasn't disappointed! Ms Biggar's characters leap off the page and become family you'll be rooting for with all your heart.

— JACQUI NELSON

I really enjoyed this romance. It has a heroine that's running around helping family, while working for the sheriff. She uses sticky notes to help keep everything straight, while the family tends to count on her to make everything right. This is full of humor and a little bit of serious in a small town type setting. I've given it a rating of 4.5. It really made me laugh.*

— NANCY LUEBKE

Twilight's Encore

What a captivating story. Twilight's Encore is the third book of Wounded Hearts series. This is Ty's and Katy's story, i have to say what a beautiful story!!!

— NICOLE- READING ALLEY

This is a very heartwarming, suspenseful book that will have you cheering for the good guys. HIGHLY RECOMMEND and Can't wait for Book 4 in the Wounded Hearts series.

— BARBARA

VALENTINE

A HEARTS AND KISSES ROMANCE

JACQUIE BIGGAR

WAVEFRONT PUBLISHING

Created with Vellum

For my Family,

If not for your encouragement, I may never have strived to become a writer.

Now, I can't imagine any occupation that could better allow me to live my dreams.

Love ya always and all ways,

Jacq

Love isn't something you find. Love is something that finds you.

— LORETTA YOUNG

FOREWORD

Val stepped closer to the crazy woman guarding her virtue with a kitchen utensil. He'd been enjoying the view for the past five minutes as she swayed to the music, her back to him while she worked at his sister's kitchen sink. Even though she wore the required hair net, he could see she was a fiery redhead, her body slim and compact beneath the wraparound apron. He should have announced himself sooner, but he hadn't expected to freak her out so badly. Normally, Sam's kitchen was a hub of activity; he was surprised to find it empty except for the pint-sized warrior.

"You can put down the weapon." He hid his amusement behind a placating smile. "I'm harmless, though my sister might be tempted to disagree. Is Sam here?"

When the woman stared at him like he was the

creature from the black lagoon, Val waved a hand in front of her eyes and grinned at the resultant snap of temper. He was right, she was a feisty one. "Sorry, I'm in a bit of a hurry. Is there a chance I could get you to answer me any time soon?"

She glared at him, threw the rubber spatula unto the counter, and swept the net from her hair, allowing the coiled layers to flow down her back. "You have a bad habit of sneaking up on people," she snapped, reddened fingers moving to untie her apron.

What was she...?

Oh.

He snapped his fingers and pointed at her. "You. The klutz that destroyed my dinner the other night. What are you doing here? Don't tell me my sister was foolish enough to hire someone who can't even hold onto a pot without it becoming a catastrophe."

Her eyes narrowed and she stared past him to the big block of knives sitting on the stainless-steel countertop. Val hurried to block her view. "Uh, uh, uh, temper, temper. You don't really want to stab me, just think of the mess."

INTRODUCTION

Take two humans who pretend they can't stand each other and one matchmaking canine and the fun is nonstop!

Val Hodgins is on the road to success. His architect firm handles some of the biggest contracts along the western seaboard. He doesn't have time to babysit his aunt's aging house or her pain in the butt dog, but when she falls ill with pneumonia he drops everything to go to her aid.

Sierra Johnson's dreams of owning a catering company go up in smoke thanks to a bad choice in boyfriends. Now, she's stuck working for a tyrannical boss, care-taking an aging townhouse, and being tormented by the owner's aggravating, caustic, way-too-attractive nephew.

Will these two get over their prejudices in time to realize love comes without a price tag?

CHAPTER ONE

Valentine wanted to kill Cupid.

"I'm just so happy you ran into me the other day, Val," Norma Jean gushed. "Otherwise we might never have met. It must be fate." She batted eyelashes at him so long and thick with black goop they left little dots under her cornflower blue eyes.

He was cursed, that's all there was to it.

"What did you say you do for a living?" he asked, making an effort to be polite.

"I'm a beautician, silly," she giggled. "Can't you tell?"

He couldn't believe he was forced to sit in a fancy-assed dining room while his date illustrated at length about her recent hair extensions and the hours, *simply hours*, it had taken to have it done. And that was after she'd shown him the new nails she called a French *man*icure. He didn't know any man who would sit through having that done to them. He smiled and nodded while shudders chased up and down his spine. The white tips looked obscene, and not in a good way. He was pretty sure those suckers could rip the flesh from a guy's back.

"It's so sweet you're helping your aunt by taking care of her house and that cute little dog," she cooed and leaned over the table, her generous breasts laid out like a banquet. Too bad he was on a female restricted diet. She eyed his arms and shoulders covered by a white linen shirt rolled up to the elbow. He could almost swear she drooled.

Lord, have mercy.

He sat back and lifted the foaming glass of beer to his lips. He was there to care for the old brownstone while his great-aunt recovered from a bout of pneumonia. And maybe convince her to sell it, if he could. She was too old to be rattling around that monstrosity on her own. He'd heard she'd been having trouble with some of the tenants, though he couldn't see it from this woman. Sugar wouldn't melt in her mouth.

"The place needs some work. Hasn't the caretaker been taking care of things?" He might as well make use of the opportunity to do a little investigating. His aunt had hired a woman to watch over the building when she went into a long-term care facility, but she'd called him last week, concerned about her precious home.

"Oh, there's a few problems," she said, batting those silly eyelashes at the male server who stopped to take their order. "I'll have the lobster bisque to start and then your seafood paella." She glanced at Val. "It's simply to *die* for."

Val had to give the younger man credit, he did a commendable job of keeping his gaze above her neckline. "Nothing for me," he said, in answer to the query. "I'm just keeping this lovely lady company."

Norma Jean—she'd told him she was named after her daddy's favorite movie star, Marilyn Monroe—pouted and flounced back in her seat, her boobs threatening a revolt in the low-cut slinky red dress. "I thought you said a date," she whined.

No, he'd said, "*It's a date.*" Not exactly the same thing.

"You seem like a very nice young woman—" he started, once again cursing Cupid under his breath, "—but I'm not a good relationship bet right now. I'm sure you understand."

Her expression went from petulant to sympathetic and she stretched across the space between them to give him a comforting hug.

"You poor man," she simpered, reluctantly releasing him to let the server set down her appetizer.

He gave Val an envious look and then turned his

attention to Norma Jean, pepper mill in hand. "Sorry for the wait, Miss. Would you like pepper for your soup?" He brandished the shaker like he was offering her a pot of gold.

Val took another sip of his beer to hide his smirk. The guy was smitten.

"Why yes, just a bit, please," she answered, smiling into his besotted gaze.

The kid waved the mill enthusiastically over her plate and fine black pepper fanned out in a graceful arc—that is until the air conditioner kicked on and the vent above their heads exploded with cold air.

Startled, the server jumped, his hands spraying the powder everywhere.

Val cursed and shot to his feet, his chair tipping over backwards. Norma Jean let out a startled shriek and flapped her hands in front of her face, causing the settling particles to again take flight. Another diner stepped forward to help, unsure of what was happening, and became the latest victim, sneezing so hard he lost his balance and hit the table, knocking the tapered candle over and lighting the tablecloth on fire.

And that's when the overhead sprinklers kicked on.

CHAPTER
TWO

By the time Sierra Johnson walked the three blocks from the bus stop to the townhouse, it had started to rain. And not a nice, gentle refreshing shower either. Nope, this storm carried winds from the north, blowing a sleet and cold rain mixture right into her face.

Seriously, this had been the day from hell.

She'd missed the darn bus this morning, which in turn made her thirty minutes late for work, and of course her boss—whom she was pretty sure hated her guts and was looking for a reason to fire her anyway—had to be in the front office when she burst through the door. She'd been forced to sit through an hour-long lecture on tardiness and its effect on the work-place environment, *blah, blah, blah* before she'd let her go with a stern warning to *never* let it happen again; or else.

It was the *or else* that got her blood boiling. What about all the extra, *unpaid*, hours she'd given the Slow Cooking Diva Catering Company? Talk about divas, Samantha Hodgins took the prize. If only Sierra could afford to start her own business and invest in herself instead of someone who didn't appreciate her efforts.

Too bad it was a pipedream.

Sighing, she opened the white gate, freckled with rust, and hurried up the uneven walk. The steps leading to the wide front porch were wet and slippery looking, but the back door was warped and refused to open in this kind of weather. She refused to consider what she would do in a fire. There wasn't much choice; rental units in the city were almost nonexistent, this was the best she could get with her limited funds, mostly because she'd agreed to be a temporary caretaker while the owner recovered from pneumonia.

She made her way up the stairs, careful to watch for ice and the soft sections in the old wood waiting to trip her up in her heels. Juggling to hold the workload she'd brought home and delve into her purse for the key, she almost missed the shivering sodden dog curled on the rug by the door. Timid brown eyes looked up at her from a whiskered face and her heart melted.

"You poor thing." She set her books down so she

could gently pat the wet head. "Who would leave you outside in this weather? You're frozen," she exclaimed.

The dog—a Dachshund—whined and turned its head to lick her fingers. Sierra glanced around, but didn't see anyone out on the street searching for their dog. "What am I going to do with you?" she murmured, checking his leather collar. A tag hung from his scrawny neck with the name *Cupid* engraved in the blue metal. It suited him. Now that he was drying she could make out a heart-shaped black patch across his back, like a saddle. He seemed healthy enough so she assumed he had to have a home.

His pathetic excuse for a tail thumped the floor.

Sierra shook her head and stood. "Come on then, let's get you dried off."

The dog didn't need a second invitation. He jumped to his stocky feet and shook, spraying cold water in every direction.

"Hey, cut that out." Sierra raised her hands to protect her clothes, though why it mattered when they were both already soaked, she didn't know.

He gazed at her expectantly, head cocked to the side. She gathered her books and unlocked the door and her new friend walked right in as though he owned the place.

"Wait for me," she called as he waddled down the hall. "I don't think pets are part of the rental agreement."

His nails rat-a-tat-tatted as he made a beeline for the kitchen at the back of the house. Sierra hurried after him, frowning at the dirty paw prints he'd left behind. How did he know where the food was? Silly question; the rich aroma of a cooking pot roast wafted down the hall. Her tummy rumbled. She'd missed lunch thanks to the terminator, otherwise known as her boss.

There were heating elements in each suite, but she'd been assured when she moved in that it was perfectly all right to make use of the main pantry, so why did she feel butterflies as she followed the little hound into the spacious room?

~

VAL OPENED the door to the brownstone and ushered Norma Jean inside. What a fiasco. He was just glad it was over.

"Thanks for accepting my apologetic dinner. My aunt's dog isn't usually so..."

"Cute?" she supplied, smiling as he helped her remove her wet coat. Of course, it had to be pouring when they left the restaurant.

"Troublesome," he corrected. Though really, he'd only been living here a week, so what did he know?

"It's strange I never saw him here before your aunt became ill." A horrified look crossed her pretty face.

"I'm so sorry, I didn't mean to bring up bad memories."

He shrugged, uncomfortable. She couldn't, he barely knew his great-aunt. "It's fine, we aren't that close." He hung her jacket by the door. "Maybe next time we go out we can avoid setting off the fire alarms."

He'd meant it as a joke, but when he turned and caught the hopeful expression in her sky-blue eyes he cursed his loose lips.

"That sounds amazing," she sighed, then glanced down the hall. "Something smells good."

Oh, hell. He'd left his roast slow-cooking while he took her out, but he hadn't planned on the delay with the water sprinklers and the firemen who wanted to know what happened. He'd be lucky if it wasn't beef jerky by now.

"Thanks," he said. "I'm stocking the freezer for those days when I don't want to cook after work. Do you want to join me for coffee and a sandwich?" he offered reluctantly.

She gazed longingly down the hall, but shook her head. "Maybe next time. I need to study, mid-terms are coming up soon."

He sighed his relief. She was nice, and would make a great friend, but he wasn't interested in anything else. He'd been burned by women enough to last a lifetime. He'd give love a pass.

"Okay, well... have a nice night," he ventured, waiting for her to go up the stairs to her room.

She laughed softly and leaned close to brush his cheek with her cherry red lips. "Don't try so hard," she murmured, before sashaying away on the stilts she wore for shoes.

Val rubbed his jaw and strode down the hall. Maybe they could just be friends.

He entered the kitchen expecting smoke, and instead found himself staring at the shapely bottom of a woman bent over his oven basting his roast while the mutt who'd ruined his day sat nearby, a sloppy grin on its narrow face.

CHAPTER THREE

Sierra inhaled the rich, beefy aroma of the pot roast and felt the stress fade away. There was nothing like good food to put a smile on the day. She carefully basted the meat, then turned off the oven. Rather than leave it to overcook and dry out, she decided to set the heavy-duty roaster on top of the stove to let the meat rest. Whoever had started the meal knew what they were doing. The scents of rosemary, garlic, and thyme made her mouth water.

Cupid whined.

She smiled down at the little dog as she stood and reached for the pot holders. "Just wait. I'll see if I can skim some off the side once I get this oven closed. It'll be our secret, okay?"

Masculine hands—much larger than her own—covered her fingers on the oven mitts.

"Let me," A deep voice rumbled. "That's too heavy for a tiny thing like you to lift." Strong arms circled her body and eased the pot from her hands.

Sierra froze. Her back was practically wallpapered to the chest of her would-be rescuer. Not that she needed rescuing. And especially not from an egotist. *Tiny little thing*—seriously? Who talked like that anymore?

Furious as she was, she held still as he set the pot on the stove, the juices in the bottom of the pan spitting and hissing. Something like she was about to do.

The moment he released her and stepped away, she whirled on him. And looked up, way up. Okay, so maybe *tiny* fit. Not that she'd admit that to him.

"Next time you might try introducing yourself before you accost a woman," she said, pleased to see the humor fade from his toffee-colored eyes. She'd never seen quite that shade before. They were... mesmerizing.

He folded muscled arms over a damp chest, the white dress shirt he wore opaque in places. Holy moly. If this were a damp t-shirt contest he'd win, hands down.

"I wasn't... accosting you, as you put it," he growled. "I was *trying* to save my roast."

Oh.

This was the creator of that gastronomic delight sitting on the stove.

Foot, meet mouth.

"Okay, well...," she muttered. "It seems you have everything under control now, so I'll get out of your way."

She awkwardly gathered up her purse and the cookbooks she'd set down earlier and attempted a graceful exit. Except... Cupid had snuck in between her feet, searching the floor with his long snout for any scraps that might have fallen. She stepped on the poor dog's tail with her heel. He yelped and scrambled to get out of the way, throwing her off balance.

"Watch out," Mr. Tall, Lean, and Grumpy yelled.

Books went one way, purse went the other. Sierra grabbed for something to save her fall and connected with the edge of the hot roaster. It tipped toward her in what seemed like slow motion, though she could already feel the tingle in her fingers and cringed at the upcoming burns to her body.

Just as the weight of the beef and liquids rolled to one side and tilted the pot in her direction an arm wrapped her waist from behind and dragged her to safety.

There was a god-awful clang as graniteware met tile. The resultant splatter brushed her legs in hot liquid, but she barely noticed. Her mouth dropped open, aghast at the mess she'd made.

"I'm so sorry," she cried. The tender meat lay on the floor looking for all the world like roadkill as Cupid slunk along the periphery, long tongue licking whatever juice he could reach.

She twisted in the stranger's arms, and met his bemused gaze. "I'll pay you back. Every cent. Which room are you renting? I'll leave the money under your door tomorrow, I promise."

~

VAL STARED down into the pixie's horrified eyes and would have laughed if he wasn't so irritated. After the day he'd had, he'd been looking forward to a nice, quiet dinner. His luck couldn't get much worse. He regretted he'd ever agreed to his great-aunt's wishes. His twin could have handled everything—she'd even offered to help—but, he'd been determined to do this on his own.

He was an idiot.

"Are you hurt?" he asked, frowning as she cradled her hand between them.

"It's nothing," she said, wriggling reddened fingertips in front of his face. "See? All good. Can you, um... let me go now?"

Strangely reluctant, he let his arms drop, surprised by the empty feeling when she stepped away. He must be hungrier than he thought.

"Do you live here?" he asked, then grimaced. Of

course, she did. Why else would she be standing in his kitchen in stocking feet? He noticed the splash marks on her shins and cursed. He grabbed a towel from the drawer, soaked it with cool water, and dropped down on one knee in front of the woman. He wrapped his hand around her calf and pressed the cloth to her leg. Her very shapely leg.

She gasped and grasped his shoulder for balance. "What are you doing?" Her breath teased the hair on his brow, sending sparks of awareness to his nerve endings.

"I'm stopping you from suing me, what do you think I'm doing?" he answered, only half joking.

She jerked backward and then tripped on the slippery floor, her hand landing with a thump on top of his head as she grabbed on to steady herself. She snatched her hand back, but not before her fingers flexed in his hair like a cat kneading a blanket.

Those sparks caught fire.

He cleared his throat and stood. She really was tiny, the top of her curly red-gold head even with his chest.

"I hadn't thought of that, thanks for the suggestion. Know any good lawyers?" She fisted her hands on her hips. Green eyes shot bolts of lightning at him, her button nose scrunched up in anger.

He lifted his hands—one holding the soiled towel — in apology. "Look, I was just trying to help. Maybe we could start again. Hi, I'm Val." He held out his hand.

She looked at him, shook her head, and walked out of the kitchen.

So, that went well.

He stared after her until a weird slurping-sliding noise caught his attention. He looked down. The Dachshund had his roast and was shaking it back and forth for all he was worth, trying to tear a chunk off.

"*Cu—pid*," Val growled.

Cupid took one look at him, sniffed, and followed the stranger out of the kitchen, a chunk of pot roast dangling from his mouth.

CHAPTER
FOUR

Val worked off his frustrations by cleaning up the mess the roast had made and washing the kitchen floor until it shone. What was he doing here? His job was demanding. He had clients waiting on their blueprints. He didn't have time to house-sit a pain-in-the butt dog, though he didn't mind staying in the brownstone. It had character. It fed his muse. Unlike the sleek and modern penthouse he owned in Vancouver, thanks to his ex-wife who'd then decided Europe was much more her *thing*.

He'd just finished dumping the mop pail and storing it away when his cell phone sang *Sweet Home, Alabama* from its spot on the counter. He turned it over to see his great-aunt's number.

"Hi, Aunty, I was just thinking about you." True

enough. Or at least how he was going to get out of caring for her mutt, anyway.

"Valentine, I can't thank you enough for taking care of my Cupid," she said, her voice a raspy whisper that tugged at his heart.

Guilt closed off the complaints he'd been about to make. It was only for a while. She'd be home soon enough. He had to believe that.

"How are you feeling?" he asked, combing tired fingers through his hair. He wondered why they came away sticky, then remembered the pixie's hands on him. She must have had some of the beef juice on her fingers. He'd have to check on her later; after he had a long, hot shower.

Aunt Alice chuckled. "About as well as to be expected with an elephant on my chest. Doctors say I should make a full recovery if I don't rush. That's what I'm calling about, actually. Can you stay on longer than we originally talked about?"

His immediate reaction was to refuse. How could he keep up to his business duties from the island? Victoria wasn't the back of beyond, but it wasn't the thriving metropolis of Vancouver either, where deals were made and broken hundreds of times a day. He needed to be there, stay on top of the pulse of the city. His success demanded as much.

But his aunt needed him.

"I was thinking... Sam said..." He stuttered to a halt, already feeling foolish for bringing it up.

"Oh, I know," she replied. He cringed while she suffered through a coughing fit. "Sorry, son," she rasped. "It's almost time for my medication. Samantha and I talked it over and we both decided you've been working too hard. This is as much for you, as it is for me."

He should have known his twin was behind this. She'd been after him to slow down for months now. Ever since Tara left him he'd been using work as an escape. But he was fine now. Great even. Ready to move on with his life and put dreams of a picket fence and two-point-five kids behind him.

Really.

"Aunty, I don't know what Sam has been telling you, but..."

"No buts." She coughed again. "Besides, are you going to say no to a sick old woman?"

She had him there.

"Of course not." He frowned at the freshly washed roaster sitting on the counter. He was stuck, there was no getting around it. "I'll stay for as long as you need me," he told his ailing aunt.

He might as well accept his fate.

CHAPTER
FIVE

Sierra backed out of The Diva's fully stocked walk-in cooler, a flat of organic farm-fresh eggs cradled in her hands. The catering company had an important client who wanted to surprise her soon-to-be daughter-in-law with a bridal shower and ordered a hundred and twenty individual cheesecakes made to look like a wedding cake. For this Saturday.

As in two days from now.

And of course, Samantha chose her for the job. Setting her up to fail so that she could be fired and have her reputation destroyed all in one fell swoop. Too bad it wasn't going to work. If there was one good trait Sierra could attribute to herself, it was tenacity. She was like a dog with a bone when faced with adversity. The Sloan's would get their cake, and furthermore, it was going to be so lovely the bride would ask for one just like it for the wedding day.

Okay—she mixed the graham crumbs, sugar and butter together and pressed it into the first of four springform pans that would comprise the base of the cake—maybe she was dreaming, just a little, but when pride's all you've got, you need it to keep your head high. Or so her mama always said. Sierra got her love of baking from her mother. She'd spent many fun-filled hours rolling dough and decorating cookies while standing on a stool pulled up to the counter next to her mom. If she closed her eyes she could still smell the vanilla scent that clung to Mama's clothes and a warm arm across her shoulders. To her, baking was a legacy of love.

She carefully placed the pans in the oven, set the timer for ten minutes, and went to work on the filling. Into the commercial stand mixer, she beat the cream cheese until fluffy, then poured sweetened condensed milk and mixed until smooth. Next came the eggs, one by one, and lemon juice. Just as she had everything blended together nicely, the timer went off and she tugged her favorite kitten-shaped mitts on, pulled the pans out of the oven, and set them on the butcher block counter. A few minutes later, the silky filling was evenly poured into the pans and returned to the oven for cooking. Time to start the next batch.

Sierra worked through lunch and was well into the

afternoon before she had enough forms made to make the display. She planned to let the cakes set up in the cooler overnight and then construct the presentation tomorrow, but she still had a couple of hours' worth of baking to get done on another order before she could call it a day.

Sighing, she flipped through her favorite radio stations on the portable player Samantha had allowed into the kitchen. She found one that played a soft rock mix and left it there, the soothing tones of Phil Collins filling the quiet room and lightening her mood. If she had to spend the next hour doing dishes, she might as well enjoy herself.

As she waited for the sink to fill and the industrial dishwasher to run through a cycle in preparation to receiving the pre-soaked pots and pans, Sierra looked out over the large workspace. Pantries lined the walls, some filled with spices and baking supplies, others filled with an assortment of bowls, measuring cups, and the small appliances that were an integral part of every kitchen. The room was painted a soft pink with white trim; a play on the company theme—The Slow Cooking Diva.

In reality, the name was a misnomer. Samantha had built the business into a thriving company with a long waiting list of happy customers by quick, professional service.

Sierra dove into the bubbles, scrubbing the bowl

from the mixer before balancing it on the tray bound for the dishwasher. She could understand her boss's dictatorial attitude—if you want to be the best at something, you have to be tough—but a little kindness goes a long way.

She had the kitchen to herself today; the rest of the crew, three cooks and Samantha, were at the Robinson's twenty-fifth anniversary gala held on their estate winery. She'd seen pictures of the spectacular venue. An outdoor tent had been set up to accommodate their guests facing the family's vineyards, with the incredible blue of the ocean as a backdrop. The menu included locally caught Sockeye Salmon, Colcannon from potatoes grown on the island, grilled broccoli with a chipotle lime butter, and for dessert—mini Meyer lemon tarts with a shortbread crust. Everything was planned down to the minutest detail, and with the catering company's reputation on the line, there was no room for error. Which is why Samantha left Sierra behind.

It hurt, there was no denying it. The only thing left to do was to prove her boss wrong. Sierra loaded the dishwasher, tugged the handle down, and stepped back from the steam escaping the closed door. She frowned at the clang-crash mixing with the noise of the water cycling through the machine; the last thing she needed was for the blasted thing to break down on her watch. Though it would certainly figure if it did; her luck was running in a downhill direction.

She stared at it for a few more moments, but nothing else happened, so she shrugged and turned to check on her cakes in the cooler.

A man leaned against the wall watching her.

Sierra let out a scream that reverberated into the rafters. She grabbed the nearest weapon, a spatula, and held it with both hands in a threatening pose, her heart fluttering like a wild thing.

"Who are you? How did you get in here? What do you want?" She'd locked the door when she came in this morning, she was almost certain she had. Hadn't she?

Oh man, oh man, she so didn't want to star in a dime-store murder mystery. *Caterer found in vat of chocolate fondant.*

The killer—stranger—stepped forward, hands out in a placating manner. "Take it easy," he murmured. "I'm here to see my sister, Samantha Hodgins?"

That voice, she'd heard that voice before. Recently. And as he stepped into the room she realized where; it was her roast beef neighbor from the townhouse. What were the chances the first guy she'd been attracted to in quite some time was related to the boss who hated her?

Oh fate, thou art a capricious beast.

CHAPTER SIX

Val stepped closer to the crazy woman guarding her virtue with a kitchen utensil. He'd been enjoying the view for the past five minutes as she swayed to the music, her back to him while she worked at his sister's kitchen sink. Even though she wore the required hair net, he could see she was a fiery redhead, her body slim and compact beneath the wraparound apron. He should have announced himself sooner, but he hadn't expected to freak her out so badly. Normally, Sam's kitchen was a hub of activity; he was surprised to find it empty except for the pint-sized warrior.

"You can put down the weapon." He hid his amusement behind a placating smile. "I'm harmless, though my sister might be tempted to disagree. Is Sam here?"

When the woman stared at him like he was the creature from the black lagoon, Val waved a hand in front of her eyes and grinned at the resultant snap of temper. He was right, she was a feisty one. "Sorry, I'm in a bit of a hurry. Is there a chance I could get you to answer me any time soon?"

She glared at him, threw the rubber spatula unto the counter, and swept the net from her hair, allowing the coiled layers to flow down her back. "You have a bad habit of sneaking up on people," she snapped, reddened fingers moving to untie her apron.

What was she...?

Oh.

He snapped his fingers and pointed at her. "You. The klutz that destroyed my dinner the other night. What are you doing here? Don't tell me my sister was foolish enough to hire someone who can't even hold onto a pot without it becoming a catastrophe."

Her eyes narrowed and she stared past him to the big block of knives sitting on the stainless-steel countertop. Val hurried to block her view. "Uh, uh, uh, temper, temper. You don't really want to stab me, just think of the mess." He wasn't reassured by the fiendish delight that filled her expression.

"Samantha is out on a catering job. Funny, she never mentioned a brother before," she muttered, treating him to an enticing glimpse of her midriff as she lifted the apron over her head.

"Yeah, well, she forgot to tell me I'd need my birth certificate when I came to work." He saw exactly when his words took root. It would have been funny if he weren't so annoyed at being tricked into helping yet another family member, even if it was his sister.

"What do you mean... work?" she growled, her posture that of a Bantam rooster, head thrust forward, nose in the air, red hair gleaming under the florescent lights.

Val leaned against the counter and crossed his arms, suddenly enjoying their little sparring match. "I mean my sister seems to think she needs help around here." He paused for dramatic effect. "I can see why now."

Yep. She's about to blow. He grinned.

She fairly crackled with aggression. Her green eyes shot sparks that ignited in her hair and created a charge he could feel vibrating across the space between them. He half expected pots to fly and the lights to short out. She reminded him of a witch—a very cute witch—ready to hocus pocus him right out of existence if she had her way. Possibly, he was messing with powers he couldn't control.

"You have a name there, Agnes?"

"It's Sierra, and you are *not* working with me," she sputtered.

Val swore he could see steam coming out her ears. "Well, *Sierra*, I beg to differ." He straightened and wandered around the room, lifting a pot here, setting a bowl down there. "If you've been employed by my sister very long, you'll know she likes to get her own way—we're nothing alike."

Sierra snorted. "Oh, I can see the resemblance," she muttered, following behind him to straighten his mess.

He turned, catching her off-guard. She gasped and jumped backward, banging against the metal shelving and setting the blender above wobbling. Val hurried forward, reaching up to steady the appliance before it toppled on her head.

The scent hit him first. An intoxicating mix of vanilla and rose petals. He took a deep breath and stilled as his chest brushed her body. He looked down into her startled expression and forgot what he'd been about to say. She had the faintest string of freckles dotting her cheek bones and highlighting thick, sandy lashes ending with silvery tips. He'd thought her eyes green the other night, but now, up close like this, he could see striations of topaz and a blue ring around the iris. Fascinating.

She cleared her throat and shifted out from under his arm, her hair licking his chest as she went. The shock of it electrified his pulse. She really was a witch; she had him under her spell.

"Thanks," she muttered, ungraciously. "But if you

didn't sneak up on people accidents like that could be avoided."

The little minx.

"You're welcome," he answered. "If you watched where you were going we could also avoid mishaps that could lead to injury. Unless, compensation is what you're after?"

She whirled to face him, hands resting on shapely hips. "Are you for real? You scared *me*, you big oaf. If anyone deserves compensation, I do... for having to put up with you."

She stomped over to the walk-in cooler and opened the door, letting a gust of chilled air sweep the room. "I have work to do. I'm sure you can see yourself out, Mr. Hodgins, or whatever your name is. I'll tell Samantha you were here." With that pronouncement, she disappeared into the cavernous depths, the door closing with a soft whoosh.

Wonder how many years he'd spend in jail for locking her in there.

CHAPTER
SEVEN

Sierra stared at the glowing white release button on the door of the cooler and tried not to panic. Why, oh why did she let her temper get the best of her? Even though it was four degrees in the cooler, sweat broke out across her brow. She could die in here and not be found until Monday morning when Samantha opened the shop. She imagined her body propped up in a corner next to the barrels of cream cheese, icicles hanging off her dainty little nose—hey, it was her daydream, she could fudge it if she wanted to—and all of her co-workers bemoaning the loss of their hardworking friend. Samantha would admit how valuable she'd been to the team and how much she'd be missed. They'd bake a cake in her honor. Shoot, now she was getting hungry on top of everything. She eyed the mini cheesecakes cooling on the shelf and regretfully turned away.

He'd left her there.

What if she couldn't get the door open and froze to death? He really was a buffoon. And they shared a rental house. The fates were certainly having a field day with her lately. Everywhere she turned, something went wrong. It was getting hard to keep her normally sunny attitude.

Who was she kidding? She'd lost that about eight months ago when her ex-boyfriend emptied their joint bank account, leaving her high and dry. He'd professed to love her, too. If that was love she'd take hate any day.

By the time she'd sorted the situation out with the credit companies and apologized hand over fist to her landlord—who'd still kicked her out—she was thousands in debt and farther than ever from making the dream of starting her own business a reality.

Tickled Pink Catering.

She had a name, a business license, even a business plan ready to take to the bank. She'd been so close; if only she hadn't bowed to Tim's soulful eyes when he'd asked why she didn't trust him enough to blend their finances. A warning light had flashed, but they'd been together for two years, so like a big dummy, she'd given in and ended up paying the price. And because it was a joint account, she had no leg to stand on with the courts when he disappeared with her money.

Lesson learned.

Never again would Sierra place her trust in a man. It wasn't worth the heartache.

The door rattled, startling her. She hesitated, picturing Hodgins with his infuriating smile on the other side. She crossed her arms and leaned against the counter, determined not to show her fear.

Samantha entered first, arms laden with bags overflowing with candy ribbons, cake decorating supplies, and a rainbow of fondant flowers on long curving stems. She looked up and met Sierra's startled stare, and frowned. "What are you hiding in here for?" She set the bags down. "Well, come on. Help us get these put away. It's been a hellishly long day. I don't need more grief," she said, turning to walk back into the kitchen.

Her obvious implication aimed at Sierra made her ears burn. Ooh, that woman.

She straightened and hurried to catch the door before it swung shut again, smiling faintly at the commiserating look from Bethany, Samantha's personal assistant. She had her arms wrapped awkwardly around a silver keg they'd filled with ice and bottled drinks for the guests wandering the estate.

Kevin followed behind, pushing a trolley overflowing with the various pieces of equipment needed to cater out-of-house, as they called off-site jobs. "Wow, you missed a swanky party, Sierra. The only thing absent was a celebrity or two." He grinned. "Then again, I did hear rumors a Kardashian might show up."

Sierra laughed, then quickly aborted it at Samantha's glare.

"If you two are finished gossiping, we have work to do," she snapped.

Kevin shrugged good-naturedly and brushed past Sierra, murmuring, "She's on the war path."

Yeah, that much was evident.

A quick search brought up no sign of her nemesis. Man, holidays at the Hodgins' house must have been a real hoot. On the one hand, you had Samantha with her mercurial temper, and on the other side her brother—shoot, she forgot to get his name—who seemed to believe practical jokes was a way of life. Never mind she'd basically pulled them on herself, he'd been little or no help either time.

His annoying voice rang in her ear, "Tell my sister I'll be back on Monday."

Wonder if she could find another job before then? Truth was, Sierra enjoyed working for the Slow Cooking Diva. The pay was good, and though she hated to admit it, Samantha was a top-notch chef who had already taught her more than all her years in culinary school. This was hands-on. If something wasn't going right, or the client changed their mind at the last minute, Samantha was quick to alter the menu to suit. That took real talent.

Sierra hurried to catch up to her boss. "I have the mini-cakes resting in the cooler for the Sloan order, I'll get it finished first thing in the morning." Samantha glanced at her like an annoying fly. Okay, then. "Do you have a minute, Sam? There's something you need to know."

Well, that got her attention.

She swung around and speared Sierra with her eyes. "Are you quitting? God, what's next? Maybe I should just go out and slit my throat, is that what you want?" The color ran up her neck and into her cheeks, then flushed away just as fast. She did a full body quiver and sank onto a nearby stool, resting her head in her hands. "I can't do this anymore. I'm done."

Sierra stared at her in shock, then glanced helplessly at Bethany and Kevin, who shrugged like it was a woman thing.

Bethany ran forward and wrapped her arm around Samantha's shoulder. "Don't talk like that. We'll work it out, we always do. Come on, honey, hold it together."

Honey?

Sierra had a hard time picturing Samantha as anyone's honey. Now her brother on the other hand...

She cleared her throat. "Umm, Sam? I think you

misunderstood. I have no plans of leaving, unless you fire me, of course." She gave a nervous laugh, but let it sputter out when Bethany raised her brow. "Truly, I like working here, ask anyone." Okay, maybe that was a mite over the top. "Actually, I just wanted to tell you your brother was here. He said he'd see you Monday."

She didn't know what she expected, but it wasn't the suicidal laughter that sprang from her boss's lips.

Wonder if she'd worked long enough to qualify for sick days yet?

CHAPTER
EIGHT

Sierra stood guard behind the four-foot cheesecake creation she'd made and watched the Sloan women and their friends smile and chatter as the bride-to-be tearfully opened gifts of every size and in a rainbow of color. Some were traditional housewarming gifts; fancy vases, bedding, kitchen utensils—everyone got a laugh out of that one. While others were more suggestive; diaphanous babydolls, teeny-tiny swimsuits for the honeymoon trip to the Caribbean, sexy bras and barely-there panties that brought a rosy hue to the bride's cheeks as she held them up between thumb and forefinger for inspection.

Sierra had called upon Kevin and Bethany to help set up the hall that ran parallel to the catering business and was regularly booked for events such as birthdays, anniversaries, wedding showers, and even the odd funeral. Today the long, narrow room was filled with peach balloons, fresh camellias and ivy, as per the family's request. It suited the bride to a T, a young blonde somewhat overwhelmed by all the attention lavished her way.

A couple of preppy country club girls strolled up to the table, martini-filled glasses tipping precariously from their fine-boned fingers.

"Is that diet cheesecake?" one asked, her green gaze suspicious above sharp cheekbones and hollowed cheeks. Her neck was so thin it barely looked capable of holding the weight of her pompous head above bony shoulders.

Well used to the whims of the health-conscious millennials, Sierra shook her head regretfully. "Sorry, we use only the finest *organic* ingredients in our baking."

Miss Anorexia's friend smirked. "She has your measure." She held out her hand. "Sandy Rivers. Ignore her, she's always like that." She dodged a pointy elbow jab to the ribs. "Have you worked for the Hodgins twins very long?"

Twins?

Samantha's brother had left that part out. And then the rest of the woman's words sank in. "They both own the catering company? I understood I was employed by Samantha Hodgins." Her stomach sank to her toes. It was like a bad segment of *Undercover Boss*.

Miss A. poked at the tired-looking olive gasping for breath in her glass. "Valentine has been gone for years. His wife insisted on the big city lights." Something in her tone suggested she and *Valentine* had a history.

At least she had a name to go with that face now. He must have been cuter as a baby because hearts and kisses was the last thing on her mind after their confrontations.

Besides, he was married.

She refused to dwell on why that bothered her. He was a temporary inconvenience—she hoped—nothing more than that.

An explosion of laughter from the crowd startled her and she dropped the pie server she'd been holding. It bounced across the table, smudging the cheesecake creation she'd just spent hours perfecting, before sliding over the side and clanging on the cement flooring.

Her cheeks burning, Sierra bent to pick up the runaway utensil, only to freeze at the sight of a pair of men's dress shoes coming to a halt near her hand. She looked up, way up, and closed her eyes in dismay.

Of course, Valentine Hodgins would be there to witness her ongoing case of the clumsies.

"I believe the customers are happier using plates, Miss Johnson," he murmured, reaching down to help her to her feet, his hand warm on her arm.

"Val." Miss Anorexia again. "We were just talking about you, sugar. It's been what, five years? What are you doing in our little neck of the woods?" She waved her half-empty glass at the group across the room. "And today of all days."

What was that supposed to mean?

Val released Sierra's arm to buss the two women's cheeks. "Sandra, beautiful as always. Gloria, mind your manners."

Gloria smiled, unperturbed. "How's Tara?"

Valentine stepped back, resuming his position on the other side of the table beside Sierra, effectively separating himself from them. "I'm sure you'd know more about that than I do," he said, eyeing the party. "Who's tying the knot?"

Gloria laughed. "You mean you haven't heard?" She handed Sandy—Sandra—her glass then clapped her hands to get the crowd's attention. "Look who's joined the party?" she called, her eyes sparking maliciously.

Even though she had no idea what all the undercurrents swirling around these three meant, Sierra knew cruelty when she saw it. As the crowd parted, allowing an unobstructed view of the blushing bride-to-be and she felt the sudden stiffening of the big body beside her, she moved closer and grasped his hand.

“Who is that?” she whispered.

“My ex-wife,” he said, his grip crushing her fingers.

CHAPTER NINE

Val couldn't believe his eyes. All this time, he'd assumed his wife—ex-wife—was gallivanting around Europe and yet here she was, in their hometown, holding up a pair of see-thru panties for a crowd of giggling women.

She looked good, damn good, actually. Her skin was a becoming pink, no doubt helped along by the bevy of teasing comments the racy underwear garnered. She wore her blond hair in a fancy bun like the ones he used to take pleasure in destroying. She'd always taken great pains with personal appearance, as though the fancy clothes and faux accent could erase her humble upbringing. He honestly hoped it did, because he hadn't been able to give her the security she so obviously needed.

Gloria picked up a dessert fork, gifted him with a

sardonic smile, and took her glass back from Sandra to give it three sharp raps with the hapless utensil. "Tara, sweetie, look what the cat dragged in." She slid her gaze over the wood nymph at his side. "No offence."

Sierra tugged free of his stranglehold and picked up a plate of her fancy cheesecake. "None taken. Cheesecake... sweetie?"

Val would have laughed except Tara chose that moment to look their way. Her expression registered the same shock he'd felt a few moments before. Her lips mouthed his name and his breath hitched with the old remembered spark of attraction. Except this time, it was fondness instead of lust that was the predominate emotion.

Hmm, maybe there was life after divorce.

He nodded toward the foyer, half expecting her to turn him down. She hesitated, smiling nervously at her family and friends who were picking up on the sudden tension in the room. Her mother glared at him like it was his fault their marriage had crumbled, while her sister sent him a flirtatious look on the sly.

"Friendly bunch," Sierra commented, setting the cake she'd offered Gloria back on the table.

He glanced down at her fiery head and something warm moved in his chest. She'd stood up for him. Even though he'd done nothing but give her grief since they first met, she'd gone to bat for him just now. She had a smear of cheesecake decorating her cheek and he reached out to remove it, relieved Gloria had been too focused on upsetting him to dig her claws into the caterer. He'd always thought Tara's friends had more than a little to do with the breakdown of their marriage. They'd blamed him for the move to Vancouver when it had been her dream all along.

"Hey," Sierra growled, swiping at his fingers. "Leave some skin, why don't you." She stepped out of his range and made busy work straightening the already pristine tablecloth. "What are you doing here, anyway? Checking up on me?" She glowered.

He noticed Tara making her way through the crowd, but now that the moment was near he was oddly reluctant to leave the little spitfire standing before him. Pieces of her fiery red hair had escaped the rigid braid she'd forced it into, and now waved about her face with a life of its own. Her green eyes glowed like the finest of Columbian emeralds against the creamy perfection of her skin while her chest heaved, betraying the nervousness she felt at his nearness. He could sympathize, parts of his body felt decidedly anxious, too. What was it about the pixie that affected him so? She was ornery, narrow-minded, opinionated, and yet loyal and kind. And incredibly sexy. That must be all it was—animal magnetism. Nothing he couldn't control.

Yeah, right.

"I am *not* checking up on you," he said, striding to

the other side of the table—and safety. "My sister asked me to stop in and see if you needed help, that's all. But—" he raised his hand to forestall the argument he could see brewing, "—I can tell you have things completely under control, so I'm going to go now." He took another step away, but couldn't leave without a final word. "Thanks. I appreciated what you did earlier. It means a lot."

Her cheeks turned pink. "Don't let it go to your head, Hodgins. I don't like bullies."

He grinned. "I'll keep that in mind. Bye, Agnes."

He turned and walked away, but not before he heard her snap, "It's Sierra, you big dope."

Yep, she was cute, all right.

Sierra watched his very fine ass as he wove through the crowded room on his way to his ex-wife. Yeah, she'd noticed the nearly imperceptible exchange between the two, who even now had disappeared, *together*, into the vestibule. She hoped no one else had picked up on their assignation, because this was an expensive soiree and the last thing she needed was for it to be a bust and have a complaint laid with Samantha. Not that it was Sierra's responsibility. No, her current sword of Damocles happened to be the boss's twin brother, and her client's ex-son-in-law. What a mess.

Gloria and Sandra stood near the far side of the table, speculation rife in the glances they kept directing between her and the closed entrance door.

"What do you suppose they're doing?" Sandra whispered, sotto voce.

Sierra was surprised they didn't have their ears plastered to the door.

Gloria stared at her as though this whole thing was her fault. "It would have been polite of you to tell Val who this party was for. Poor man, it must have been a shock."

One that Miss Blabbermouth was happy to impart.

Sierra gave a careful shrug, while inside her blood was boiling. If his ex was anything like her friends, Hodgins was well rid of them!

"I work for Samantha. I had no idea her brother would even be here today, much less who his affiliations are. Now, if you'll excuse me?" She gave a false smile before gratefully turning away to serve a matronly woman.

"Did you do this beautiful display, dear?" an elderly lady asked, her expression knowing as she eyed the disgruntled two who'd moved aside for the seniors. The twinkle in the older woman's eyes implied conspiracy, drawing a genuine smile from Sierra.

"I did. This is a new design I came up with just for Mrs. Sloan."

The senior laughed. "That's me." She held out her hand. "Martha Sloan, the bride-to-be's grandmother. You must be talking about my daughter-in-law, Bernadette. She mentioned she'd found a talented young caterer."

Sierra was charmed by the kindly old lady. Maybe there was hope for Tara yet. "Thank you. You must be excited for your granddaughter's wedding. She looked like she was having a good time today."

"Tara?" Martha glanced around as though unaware that she was in the middle of a secret tryst with her ex-husband. "Oh, yes. She was married once before, but they weren't really suited. She loves Andrew very much. I'm sure they will be very happy together. Don't you agree, Gloria?"

Gloria, startled at the sound of her name, spilled vermouth down the front of her silk dress. "Shi...," she glanced at Mrs. Sloan, then grabbed a napkin from the table to dab ineffectively at the mark. "Shoot, I hope this doesn't stain."

"A little hydrogen peroxide and baking soda will take care of it," Sierra said, earning a glare for her efforts.

"Yes, well, we better get to it then," Gloria muttered. "Tell Tara we'll call her later, will you, Mrs. Sloan?"

"Of course, dear. Say hi to your mother. I haven't seen her in a while."

"Yes, ma'am." She speared Sierra a knife-edged glance before giving Sandra a very unsubtle shove. "It was nice to see you, again."

"You too, my dear." Martha grinned as they trounced away. "Nice girls."

Sierra wanted to hug the diminutive dynamo. Now they were alone, curiosity rose. "So, you knew your granddaughter's first husband?" She rubbed her goose-pebbly arms, feeling his sardonic eyes on her though he was nowhere near.

"Valentine? He's a good boy. Too lenient for my Tara, she needs a heavy hand, if you know what I mean. She didn't have it easy as a youngster and now I think she's trying to make up lost time. Andrew will be good for her. Keep her in check."

Sympathy rose. Hodgins must have loved his wife very much. He'd uprooted himself, did everything he could to please her, and still ended up alone.

She glanced toward the still closed foyer doors and frowned. What were they doing out there?

CHAPTER TEN

Val followed his ex-wife into the vestibule of the Slow Cooking Diva's banquet room, and wondered what he could say that hadn't already been said. The last time he'd seen Tara she was boarding a jet to Paris, tears streaming from blue-bonnet eyes. He'd felt like the bad guy even though he'd done everything in his power to make their marriage last. It wasn't her fault. Love was a two-way street and it turned out theirs was a dead end. He honestly hoped she had better luck the second time around. She deserved it.

"I guess I should apologize," she murmured, turning to face him in the light streaming through the floor-to-ceiling window. "I could have let you know I was back in the country."

And getting hitched.

"You don't owe me any explanations," Val admitted, "though it would have been nice not to get blindsided like this. What made you choose The Diva for your wedding shower?"

"Samantha is the best. Just because we aren't together anymore, I didn't see any reason not to give her the contract." She smiled and tipped her head. "Was that wrong of me?"

She was right, he was being petty. "No, I'm sure she appreciates the business. I just didn't expect to see you here, back home."

After spending thousands to set her up in a fancy Paris apartment, but he kept that to himself.

"I know. Crazy, isn't it?" She twirled, arms outstretched as though to catch the rays of the sun. "I met Andrew at that quaint little bistro near the park. You know, the one we liked so much on our honeymoon?" She had the grace to look chagrined at the memory. "Anyway, we hit it off right away. Imagine my surprise to learn he came from Victoria. I mean, what are the chances?"

What, indeed.

"You look happy," he said, anxious to end the dance with the past.

"Oh, Val, I am. We have so much in common. It's... effortless, you know?" She came closer, laid a hand on his arm. "Not like you and me. We had to work at being happy, we just didn't realize it at the time." She stared into his eyes. "What about you, Valentine? Are *you* all right? Who's the pretty woman catering our function? I swear I could feel the sparks between you from across the room."

He could feel his ears grow warm, as though he were a callow youth with his first crush. Just because he found the little pixie cute, it didn't mean he was planning on doing anything about it. He didn't even live on the island anymore, it would never work. But the thought of taming the vixen heated more than his ears.

"Ha," she laughed. "I was right. You *are* hooked on the caterer!"

He glanced over his shoulder, half expecting Sierra to be standing there with a look of shocked horror on her expressive face. It wasn't like they got along, though there'd been an awareness between them from the day they met. If only she wasn't doing such a poor job caring for his great-aunt's home. Sooner or later, he was going to have to talk to her and he wasn't looking forward to the confrontation.

His gaze came back to Tara. He shook his head, well aware of her penchant for matchmaking. "No, don't even think about it. Just because you've found happily-ever-after with your Andrew, it doesn't mean the rest of us are looking."

She looked stricken. "Val, I'm sorry we didn't work out. I love you, I'll always love you. I'm just not *in* love with you. It took me a long time to figure out the distinction, but it's all the difference in the world, isn't it?"

"I love you, too." He pulled her close and kissed her forehead. She was the smart one in their relationship. She'd known when to let go. "Be happy," he whispered.

CHAPTER ELEVEN

"Well, isn't this cozy?"

Sierra heard the sarcastic words and the gasp from the crowded room. She turned from the cooler she'd been rummaging through to see the foyer doors flung wide and a suspiciously pleased-looking Gloria standing nearby. But that wasn't the worst of it; she'd caught Hodgins and the bride-to-be in a torrid clinch!

"Oh, dear. Oh, dear," Martha muttered, hands clenched to her ample bosom. "This isn't good, not good at all."

She could say that again.

What was Hodgins thinking? Sierra frowned. He was going to get her fired. The man was a consummate flirt. She should have known he wasn't really interested in her. She refused to analyze why she had the urge to curl up in a ball and cry over the loss. The only thing that mattered right now was damage control.

She circled the table and hurried toward the entry, stopping just long enough to give Martha a quick hug. "Don't worry, I'll fix it." She wasn't sure how, but Hodgins *wasn't* going to ruin this family celebration—not on her watch.

By the time she pushed through the gathering throng to the doorway, the lovebirds had split apart, looking suspiciously guilty.

Gloria smirked. "Looks like your boyfriend isn't as over his ex-wife as he may have suggested."

Sierra glared. "He's not my..." *boyfriend. That's it.*

Before she could second-guess the impulsive nature that had gotten her in trouble more times than she could count, Sierra pinned a loving smile on her face and slipped by the piranha to slide up next to Hodgins.

She ran a proprietary hand up over his admittedly very nice abs and brought it to rest on his chest, smiling into narrowed cinnamon eyes. "There you are, darling. I was just telling your ex-wife's grandmother about our little cooking adventure at home. You were so funny." She laughed and patted tensed muscles, her own nerves squirming.

"That's right, she was." Martha's relieved voice from over Sierra's shoulder told her she was doing the right thing.

Tara looked confused. "You live together?" she asked.

"Well...," Val started, his hand coming up to cover Sierra's. A shiver whispered up her spine.

"Hodg... Valentine, didn't want me to say anything, but I couldn't help myself. He's just so sweet, isn't he?" She was going to give herself a toothache with all this sugar-talk.

He squeezed her fingers in warning. "I didn't think this was the appropriate time to bring it up, *sweetheart*," he corrected. He bestowed a warm smile on Tara. "This is your day."

"I can't believe Samantha didn't mention it," Tara said, her tone uncertain, "but, I'm happy for you." She stared at her ex-husband, then shifted her gaze to Sierra. "Both of you."

Great. Now that her actions had overshadowed their scene, Sierra was ready to get the heck out of there. "Well, I better get back to work. I don't want to get fired," she said, only half joking as she worked to pry her fingers from his grasp.

"Honey, can I have a word before you go?" Val asked, tugging her hand up and bestowing a slow, sensuous kiss to her palm.

At the first trace of his breath, and then his lips on her skin, Sierra froze. Goosebumps skittered from the touch of his mouth, down her arm, and settled deep in her chest to bounce against her heart. She panicked, her pulse going into full on fight or flight momentum. She yanked her hand free and jumped back a few paces, releasing a nervous laugh that came out more like a squawk. Her palm felt as though he'd branded her as his property. She had to fight the urge to scrub it on her skirt—except everyone was already staring at her as though she'd lost her mind.

They weren't far off.

"She looks scared," Gloria sneered. "What did you do to the poor kid?"

Who's she calling a kid? Sierra stiffened and just barely refrained from balancing on her toes. She'd always hated her short stature and youthful complexion. In school, she'd dreamed of becoming the *femme fatale* instead of the girl next door. Time had rid her of most of those fantasies, but every now and then—like now—the old envy bug bit.

"Gloria, your fangs are showing." Val smiled as he spoke, taking the sting out of his words.

Tara moved to her friend's side and gave her a hug. "Ignore him, he gets grumpy in crowds." She turned them toward the reception hall. "Let's give these two some privacy, shall we?"

They joined the slow throng moving toward the double entry doors. Sierra started after them, gasping when a strong arm wrapped around her waist, pulling her off-balance and up against an immovable object. Hodgins.

CHAPTER TWELVE

Val sucked in a breath as Sierra's back crashed into his chest. He lifted his chin just in time to avoid a collision with her head. The woman was a walking, talking catastrophe waiting to happen. One who smelled like a decadent pastry and felt like a ray of sunlight in his arms—warm and beckoning.

They stood there, barely moving, until the party-goers disappeared. Tara turned to close the doors on her way out and gave him a pensive smile. Their relationship might have had its ups and downs, but at one time they'd loved one another enough to get married. The hurt and anger he'd carried for so long dissipated, leaving fondness and a genuine hope for her happiness. He answered her smile with one of his own.

The moment the door clicked shut, Sierra whirled

in his arms, her eyes crackling with green fire. "What are you doing?" she snapped. "You're going to give them the wrong idea."

Val laughed, he couldn't help it. "I think you already did that with your acting debut, *darling. Remember our little cooking adventure at home?*" He repeated, throwing her words back at her. "I don't know what your aim is, but half of Victoria will think we're an item by tonight."

Her neck turned red, the flush blossoming up to cute apple cheeks. She reached behind her back and pried his fingers loose, putting a yardstick worth of distance between them. "I was *trying* to help." She stared at him. "You don't know, do you?"

He frowned. There was nothing he hated worse than feeling like an fool, something this woman seemed able to accomplish with a twitch of her dainty little nose. "Know what, that you are an annoying pain in the butt?"

She snorted. "Takes one to know one, buddy. No, that your ex-wife is marrying Councilman Bosemann. As in, Victoria's mayoral candidate, Bosemann." She tapped his chest. "I seriously doubt your sister could afford the fallout if this bridal party were a bust. I was just doing damage control, that's all."

A Councilman. That explained a lot. Tara always did have her eye on the prize. He could look at it objectively now, but there'd been a time when her hunger for respectability had driven an insurmountable wedge between them. And now, here was another woman he was interested in who was worried about appearances. He sure could pick 'em.

"Well... say something," she demanded, hands fisted on slim hips and chin in the air.

"What's for dinner?"

"I know I should have stayed out of... what?" She stuttered to a stop and stared at him like he was an idiot.

Maybe she was right, but the more he thought about it the more her *faux pas* seemed like a lifesaver. The last thing he wanted or needed was sympathetic looks from family and friends who knew about Tara's upcoming marriage. With Sierra as a buffer, he could save face—at least until he went back to Vancouver.

"It's going to be impossible to explain your screw-up—" he grunted as she poked his midriff, "—so I figure I'm obliged to play along and save you some embarrassment." He grinned at her outraged look. "Besides, you owe me a dinner."

LORD, she was an idiot.

She'd gotten herself into some messes lately, but this was a doozy. And it all came back to Hodgins. His sister's catering company. His ex-wife. His tall, well-muscled body and charismatic smile. His annoying sarcasm. He was beginning to permeate every area of her life. She worked with him, lived in the same house as him—heck, she was even dreaming about him.

Her cheeks burned.

She jerked her thoughts back to the issue at hand. The one he'd instigated by following his ex into this room. But, it didn't matter. If there was one thing she was good at, it was problem-solving.

She could fix this.

"Okay, this is what we're going to do," she said, pacing back and forth in thought. "You go talk to your sister so she knows what's going on, and I'll pack up and field any questions." She glanced at him on her way by to gauge his reaction, but he was frowning at her feet. She looked down. Now what? Maybe her clogs weren't super fashionable heels like these women preferred, but they were comfy and didn't leave her limping for hours after a long day on her feet.

"Are you listening to me?" she growled, suddenly uncomfortable with her fashion choices.

He jerked his chin. "*What* are you wearing?"

See, she knew he was a barbarian.

"Shoes. Why, you never seen them before? Let's get back on topic, please. You. Talk to Samantha. I'll hold down the fort here. Later, we'll go out somewhere public for dinner—" she scrunched her shoulders, prepared for another scathing remark "—and then we can pretend this was all a bad dream. Deal?"

He looked at her for a long moment, then walked over and tipped her chin up to meet his gaze. "I appreciate you stepping in to protect my virtue today, Agnes. No one's ever done anything that nice for me before. You're okay, you know that?"

A warm glow washed over her chest. Damn, she didn't want to like this guy.

"Now how about we seal the deal with a kiss?" he whispered.

Her heart hitched a ride with her breathing, skidding to a halt in case he changed his mind. "Well, get on with it then," she muttered, determined to play it cool.

He met her mouth with a smile on his lips. *It tickles*, she thought fleetingly before the pressure changed and she went weak in the knees. Holy tamale. She grabbed his shoulders and hung on in a world that suddenly became all about the senses. His skin rasping her cheek. The scent of soap and woodsy cologne and man. The taste of his tongue as it moved against hers in a sensuous dance she wanted never to end. The feel of his hands moving restlessly up and down her sides. His thigh brushing her stomach and the achy want only he could stop.

"Hodgins," she breathed.

He lifted his head to stare into her eyes. "Say it, Sierra. I want to hear my name on your lips."

She hesitated, feeling as though some indefinable threshold was about to be crossed. "Valentine," she said, sighing. "This is a mistake."

He bent down and softly kissed her swollen lips. "Probably," he agreed. "But, at the moment, I don't particularly care."

CHAPTER THIRTEEN

Sierra didn't see Valentine for the next few days. She'd been grateful to Tara and her grandmother for ending the party early, thereby saving her the gauntlet of questions from Val and Tara's friends and family.

Martha had hugged her on the way out, saying, "He's a good man, dear. Give him a chance."

It seemed strange there was no animosity between the two families, but then, she only had her own personal experience to draw upon. When her father divorced them, her mother had cried for months afterward. That's how Sierra thought of it—them. Considering she'd never seen him after the divorce, it wasn't too surprising. Whenever her mother would see something, or hear a certain song, or cook his favorite meal, it would all start up again. Small wonder Sierra had a bad case of commitment phobia.

If only she could quit thinking about Valentine Hodgins.

She lined the nail gun up with the edge of the new deck planking and pulled the trigger. The weather had finally changed enough for her to tackle some of the repairs on the old townhouse. Samantha had given her a few days off after the busy weekend—totally unlike her—so Sierra was taking advantage of the time. And no, she wasn't hanging around home hoping a certain six-foot-whatever guy would show up and make her dinner and pretend they were a couple and kiss her and...

Really, she wasn't.

A hammer would be more satisfying, but the nail gun recommended by the hardware shop really got the job done. She gazed back at the work she'd accomplished and grinned. Another hour or two on the planking and she could start the painting. By this evening the front porch would be finished.

When she accepted the caretaker position she hadn't realized just how much work would be involved. At first, she'd planned on hiring it out, but the owner was a sweet old lady in hospital recovering from a bout with pneumonia. The last thing she needed was extra expenses when Sierra was perfectly able to do the job herself. Well, her and YouTube.

Amazing what you could learning watching how-to videos.

She wriggled on her knees until her toes dangled over the newly repaired step, and then stretched to get a nail into the second to last plank. The satisfying blast from the air gun almost, but not quite, muffled a strange choking sound from behind. Sierra glanced over her shoulder and gasped, nearly sending a nail into the wall at the same time.

Valentine stood on the sidewalk leading up to the front door, his gaze trained on her backside. "Do you have a license for that thing?" he asked.

Outraged, Sierra turned and plopped on the aforementioned *'thing'*. "What are you doing sneaking up on a girl that way?" she demanded, tugging the hem of her shorts down. It had been so warm when she got up this morning she'd decided to give her legs some sun. She regretted that move now.

"Don't mind me." He laughed. "I was enjoying the view." She lifted the nail gun in a threatening manner and he took a hasty step back. "I was talking about the gun, though both could be regarded as lethal weapons."

His disarming smile invited her to share in the joke and Sierra caved like the rotten boards she'd just replaced. The man was too charismatic to resist.

"You're looking a little flushed there, Miss Johnson. Would you like a hand?"

Hand, shoulder, mouth, she was willing to take whatever he offered. Darn hormones.

She scrambled to her feet and used a paint rag from her back pocket to wipe the moisture from her brow. “Not all of us can spend the day lollygagging, Hodgins. Shouldn’t you be helping your sister since she gave me some bonus days off?”

He shook his head. “Don’t worry about Sam, she wouldn’t have done it if she couldn’t spare you. Besides, she told me your cheesecake creation won her another three accounts for the summer. Well done, Sierra.”

If she wasn’t blushing before, her face was positively on fire now. Funny what a few words from a handsome guy could do to a girl’s equilibrium.

“I was just about to take a break. Want to have a glass of ice tea?” She pointed to a glass jug filled with amber liquid, ice and lemons, and a plate sitting on ice piled with sandwiches waiting on a table she’d set up under the cherry tree.

He raised a brow. “Were you planning on feeding an army?”

She shrugged, embarrassed. It had started as a light lunch, but then she couldn’t decide between tuna or chicken and ended up making two of each and quartering them into elegant little bites. It wouldn’t go to waste, she could wrap the plate and place it in the fridge. The other tenants would appreciate the effort.

"Construction is hard work." She bent and brushed the dust and wood chips from her knees, grimacing at the ugly marks left behind. When she straightened, it was to find him studying her again, his eyes dark and watchful. Awareness arced between them and it was as though his hands were on her tingling breasts. Her lips parted, the pulse pounding in her ears like a winter storm surge.

Confused, Sierra turned and led the way across the yard, anxious for a breathing space from those perceptive eyes. She poured two glasses of ice-cold tea and picked one up to hold against her cheek, praying for a bit of sanity.

Val leisurely followed her across the lawn, glancing up at the cherry tree on his way. "Won't be long now before this old girl blooms. I remember climbing it as a kid." He grinned.

"I totally see you as a precocious child. It seems so strange that most of the country is under snow and we're out here having a picnic." Then it occurred on her what he'd said. "You climbed *this* tree as a child?"

Val met her gaze and slowly nodded. "It seemed much bigger back then."

Sierra frowned. "Did you live here, or have friends who lived here? Why didn't you mention this before?"

"Like when? We haven't exactly been on the best of terms. And anyway, it's in the past. It doesn't matter, right?" He picked up a sandwich and then set it down again. “I had family who lived here,” he admitted. “But it’s been years since I’ve been back.”

“So that’s why you rented a room? You wanted to see if it was the way you remembered it?”

He looked at the house, resting like a graceful old lady in the warm spring sun. “Yeah, something like that.”

When he turned back Sierra could feel the distance between them though they were only inches apart, and she regretted the loss. Whatever was bothering him, she wanted to help.

She just didn’t know how to ask.

CHAPTER

FOURTEEN

Val regretted mentioning his connection to the house. Sierra was understandably curious, but if he admitted he was there to check up on *her,* it would ruin any chance they had of a relationship.

And he wasn't ready to let that go.

She looked edible in blue jean shorts and a blue-green ribbed t-shirt that picked up the striations in her eyes. She'd tamed her fiery red hair into a ruthless braid that trailed down the center of her back and filled him with the urge to wrap it around his fist and draw her close. So close he'd feel her breathing as though it were his own. He thought of the moment he'd held her at Tara's wedding shower a hundred times since it happened. Even though Sierra was a foot shorter, she'd fit against his chest as though she was an extension of his body. It should have felt strange, even wrong, to kiss another woman with his ex in the next room, but Sierra tempted him beyond reason. She appealed to him physically, but it was more than that. She was smart, funny, loyal—he'd seen the long hours she worked to make Sam's business a success—and kind.

There was a lot about Sierra Johnson to like.

"So, are you just here to check my progress, or did you show up to help?" she teased.

Val's pulse jumped. Did she know? But then he noticed the gleam in her eye and he smiled. "I've been known to lift a hammer now and then." He took a better look at the work she'd done so far—now that her delectable body wasn't distracting him—and had to admit she was doing a good job. The deck would be much sturdier, and safer, by the time they were done.

"I just need to give Samantha a call and then I'm all yours," he said, turning away to phone his sister, but not before he caught the rosy flush on Sierra's cheeks. He felt an answering warmth in his gut. Damn, he liked making her blush.

"Where are you?" Sam's growl in his ear had the smile fading from his lips.

"I'm home. I told you I needed to check on the pooch." Not that he'd done so yet. He was actually surprised Cupid wasn't outside begging for the sandwiches Sierra had made. The dog was a walking garbage can.

"I didn't realize it was going to take all day," she snapped.

Val held the phone away from his ear and frowned at the picture of Sam on the screen. He'd taken it three years ago, just before...he raised the phone, "Shit Sam, it slipped my mind this is your anniversary. I'll be there right away. Tell Bethany it's my fault."

It took his sister years of turmoil before she met and fell in love with her life partner. When the Federal law changed to allow same sex marriages in two thousand-five it was the catalyst she needed to admit her sexuality. Their parents had taken it better than she'd expected, and when she'd come to him with the news all he could say was, "It's about damn time."

Sam sighed, the sound a noisy gust of air. "It's not you, it's me. I should have planned something special, and I didn't. I've been so caught up in the business lately, I've let the important things slide." She went silent for a minute and he glanced over his shoulder. Sierra was crouched by an open can of paint, patiently stirring the oils to mix the shade to the right consistency. She looked up, met his gaze, then returned her attention to the can, leaving him oddly unsettled. "Listen, take the afternoon off. You're only here for a short time, go out and enjoy the day. We'll catch up tomorrow, okay?"

"Sure, whatever works for you," he murmured, her words ringing in his ears. "Now go remind that wife of yours why she agreed to marry you." He hung up on her laughter and slowly pocketed his phone. She was right, he was leaving soon. It would be irresponsible to get involved with Sierra, only to walk out on the relationship. He caught her peeping at him while tipping the paint into the roller tray and his stomach knotted. How did she turn him on with just a glance? He thought about making an excuse and getting out while he could, but then she dripped some paint on her sneaker and cursed her clumsiness and he was lost.

"You won't have enough for the house if you keep that up." He grinned.

"Put your paintbrush where your mouth is, Hodgins," she replied with an answering smile.

How could he say no to a challenge like that?

"How about a friendly wager, Agnes?" He loved how her chin came up every time he used that silly nickname on her. If she was half as tempestuous in bed... He cleared his throat. "I'll take the left side of the deck, you do the right. Last one done cooks dinner. Deal?" He held out his hand and tried for an innocent look. She didn't need to know he'd painted his share of houses in the early days of his career.

She eyed him suspiciously, before thrusting her hand into his and giving a brisk shake. "I like pasta," she quipped.

CHAPTER
FIFTEEN

Sierra heated oil in a large frying pan, then added chopped onions, bacon, mushrooms and a drop of butter for flavor. She stirred briskly until the bacon was crisp and the mushrooms tender. The rich scents filled the kitchen and caused her tummy to rumble. Smiling, she added cream, brought it to a boil, then left it to simmer until the sauce thickened. Meanwhile, she reached into the toaster oven and flipped the garlic herb bread she planned to serve with the meal.

"Almost ready," she called, pleased. If she had to lose the bet, at least he wouldn't be able to complain about the meal.

"Good, I'm starving," Valentine said, walking into the room holding a bottle of wine. "I thought a glass of

Italian Chianti would pair well with the dish. Interested?"

Um, yeah.

More than she wanted to admit. He totally rocked the sexy handyman look in faded blue jeans and a chambray work shirt rolled up muscular forearms.

"What?" he asked, gazing at her quizzically as he released the cork on the bottle with a soft *pop*.

She startled, flustered at getting caught staring. "Is that paint in your hair?" She pointed to the left side of his head, hoping to defuse his suspicions.

It didn't work. He slowly set the wine down and wandered across the kitchen, reminding her of a big cat stalking its prey. His tawny hair glinted under the soft overhead lighting and she shuddered with the urge to run her fingers through its thickness.

And then she got her wish.

He stepped into her space, so close she could smell the soap he'd used to wash up with after their painting sprint and the warmth emanating from that big body. Wonder if he'd mind if she burrowed under his arm like a kitten seeking a blanket? Though, if the look in his eyes were anything to go by, offering comfort and shelter was the last thing on his mind.

He crowded Sierra against the counter, his hands resting on her hips. The countertop dug into her back, but she barely noticed, her focus on thick shoulders, a brawny chest, and the solid leg wedging hers apart. Talk about stuck between a hard place and...

"Wanna look?" he murmured next to her ear.

She jerked like a puppet on a string. "Wha...? Oh." She stared, her eyes wide, as he turned his head so she could check for the supposed paint splotches. She couldn't help it, she giggled. For a second there she thought he was propositioning her. Then he turned and caught her giggles with his lips.

Sierra froze. The taste of Valentine was better than the most decadent chocolate soufflé. He groaned as though he felt the connection as well. His lips teased and tempted until she opened to him, lost to the man holding her like she was precious to him. His hands left the counter to roam restlessly up and down her sides, working her shirt free of her shorts. Then he was underneath and it felt so amazing to have his skin on hers that she wanted it all, everything he had to offer.

Greedy, she wrapped her arms around his neck, her fingers toying with the still-damp curls. He lifted her to sit on the counter and she gasped, the lights strobing in front of her dazed eyes.

"Better," he rasped, his mouth nibbling the line of her jaw to her ear. "I've been dreaming of this for weeks. I can't get you out of my head."

Even as her pulse pounded in anticipation, her heart thrilled with his confession. He cared. Why else would he have spent the day helping and couldn't seem to keep his hands off her? Sex, obviously. Most red-blooded males wouldn't say no if it was offered, and she wasn't exactly calling foul. But, this felt like more. They laughed at the same jokes, liked the same food, enjoyed each other's company. They had a bond.

And right now, as he nibbled his way down her neck, she ached with the need to lie with him, to prove how he affected her in the most elemental way a woman could. But that would be a mistake.

"Val... Valentine stop," she panted, her fingers curling into his shirt. "We need to talk."

"Sure, honey," he muttered, his hands on her breasts. "Later."

Her head fell back, the touch of his lips blowing every coherent thought out of her head. Okay, she'd given common sense her best shot. Time to enjoy the moment and worry about the consequences later.

"What's that smell?" A voice called from down the hall.

Sierra blinked the room back into focus, her nose wrinkling at the charred scent of scalded milk. Belatedly, she remembered the carbonara sauce simmering on the stove and she pushed against Val's broad shoulders—flushing as he tugged her shirt down before backing away. His hair looked as though he'd been through a wind storm, but there was no time to warn him before one of the tenants breezed into the room, her gaze narrowing on the scene she'd interrupted.

"Norma Jean," Val greeted the woman, his smile a little vague. Before Sierra could read too much into that though, he was stepping between them to usher the pretty blonde out. "I've been meaning to call you and rebook our dinner, but my sister keeps me busy at her catering company. Have you heard of it, The Slow Cooking Diva?"

"Oh yes," Norma Jean gushed, trying unsuccessfully to peek over his shoulder. "My cousin used her for her wedding last year. The food is scrumptious. But wait... aren't you here to help your Aunt Alice straighten out the management trouble with the brownstone?"

If betrayal were a color, it would be gray.

The butter-yellow walls, cheerful apple canisters, hardwood floors. All of it faded away. Sierra felt the words like daggers piercing her flesh. He'd used her. He didn't care about her. All he wanted was to catch her not doing her job so he could get her fired. And apparently, he hadn't wasted any time getting to know the other females in the building.

She was a fool.

He glanced back as she slid off the counter, the landing jarring some belated sense into her head. His eyes pleaded with her to understand. She raised her chin and turned away to shut off the stove before the smoke alarm went off, though it would serve him right.

She may have lost the bet, but the war had just begun.

CHAPTER
SIXTEEN

By the time Val escorted Norma Jean back to her room, dropping a lot of non-answers along the way, and returned to the kitchen, Sierra was long gone. He sighed. Guess it was too much to hope she would have granted him the benefit of a doubt.

He filled the sink and took his frustration out on the hapless frying pan. He'd looked forward to dinner with her more than he'd cared about anything for a very long time. The worst of it was that it was his own damn fault. If he'd come clean with her from the start, this never would have happened. He frowned. Maybe it was for the best. He wasn't looking for another relationship, and Sierra had *complicated* written all over her delectable body.

He threw the cloth into the sink, ignoring the

resultant splash, and planted his hands on the edge of the counter. He was instantly reminded of Sierra's hips between his arms, her sweet taste and wanton touch. The woman had slid beneath his skin. She was spunky, sassy, and so sexy she lit his blood on fire.

Was he really going to let her walk away?

Hell, no.

He turned and almost tripped over the little dog staring at him with fathomless brown eyes. "Cupid, where have you been hiding?"

He crouched and rubbed the floppy ears. "I suppose you heard all that," he said, comforted by the thin tail sweeping the floor. "I screwed up, big time. Got any advice?"

Cupid whined, licked his hand, and trotted to the back door. When Val didn't move fast enough, he rose on his haunches and scratched at the wood with his front paws.

"Hey, cut that out," Val growled, glaring at the gouges. "Give a guy a minute to get there, why don't you?" Damn mutt. He'd managed to get himself in and out with no trouble before, what was with the sudden helpless routine?

He rose and hurried to open the door so the dog could go and do his business, and that was when he saw the vision—an ethereal figure silhouetted against a backdrop of ghostly branches and a twilight sky.

Sierra.

Cupid whined again, and Val glanced down to see the animal staring up at him with a *What are you waiting for?* expression in his intelligent eyes.

Go figure. The dog was smarter than he was. It stood to reason she'd stepped outside. As mad as she'd been—he would have heard if she'd followed him down the hall earlier. What was he going to say?

Start with an apology, dummy.

Startled, Val stared at the hound—who stared right back. Okay, he was losing it. Dogs don't talk. But he was right, Sierra deserved an apology.

He hurried back to the kitchen, poured each of them a glass of wine, then had to fiddle to get the door unlatched. How come this always looked more romantic in the movies? He was afraid she'd be gone by the time he got out the door, but no, she was still there, head tipped to the side, a secret smile tilting full lips as she watched his juggling act.

"And I thought I was the clumsy one." She laughed, then gasped when he nearly spilled the alcohol while avoiding the mutt squeezing between his feet. "Watch out for Cupid," she warned.

"What about me?" Valentine muttered.

"You deserve to fall on your face, the dog is innocent," she said as he handed over the fragrant wine.

Val disagreed, but he was learning to pick his battles. She reminded him of a fairy by moonlight. He was afraid if he touched her she'd disappear, the mere thought enough to stop his heart. Maybe she did know magic, for she'd certainly placed a spell on him—one he wasn't anxious to cast off.

"Are you chilled?" She'd changed into a dark blue hoodie earlier, but those shapely legs of hers were still bare. He couldn't tell if they had goose bumps though.

"Are you staring at my legs?" she asked, amusement ripe in her voice.

At least she hadn't thrown the wine in his face—yet.

"I was trying to see if you were cold, but yes. It's kind of hard not to stare at perfection."

She ducked her head at his words, but not before he saw her smile. "Smooth, Hodgins, very smooth. No wonder you have all the women chasing you."

Heat prickled his neck. He'd always gotten along with the fairer sex, that was true, but he genuinely meant everything he'd said to her. She was perfect, even with that rebellious attitude of hers.

"The difference is—" He caught a few strands of wayward hair and tucked them gently behind her ear, suppressing a groan when she shivered at his touch. "—I'm not chasing them." Unable to resist any longer, he leaned down and laid his mouth on hers, teasing her lips until she opened to him on a soft moan that went straight to his heart. She'd drank some of the wine he'd brought and her lips tasted of cherry. Smoky. Warm. Inviting. He punctuated each thought with a taste, losing himself in the lushness of her mouth.

By the time he eased back, they were both breathing hard. He took comfort from the fact she seemed as affected by their chemistry—which was off the wall—as he was. "Why didn't you wait for me back there?" he asked, trying to read her expression in the dim light. "I wanted to explain."

She stiffened and pulled away from his arms. He shivered.

"There's nothing to say," she said. "You're here to protect your family, and I'm here doing my job. Or trying to," she muttered. "It would have been nice to hear your connection to the house from you though, instead of Bedtime Barbie in there."

"Norma Jean is actually pretty nice, you'd probably get along." She glared and he hastily added, "Not that it matters." He grasped her elbow when she would have turned away, careful not to slosh the wine. "Look, I'm sorry. I should have come clean from the start. I have no excuse, other than I really was trying to help my poor great-aunt who's lying sick in the hospital." He gazed at her with a winning expression. "Forgive me?"

Slowly, she shook her head. "Wow, you're good. No wonder your mother named you Valentine." She gazed up at the blanket of stars above their heads, her slender throat on display, before releasing a heartfelt sigh and sinking to the ground at his feet. "Any other secrets you care to share?"

Relief loosened the vise on his chest. She was giving him a chance. He handed her his glass of wine and ran into the house, returning with a woven throw he found on a chair in the lounge. He draped it over her legs, then sat on the grass at her side.

"Thanks," she murmured. "That was sweet of you."

He wasn't feeling sweet. If she knew what he was thinking she'd probably run for the hills. But then, she laid her head on his shoulder and all those X-rated thoughts morphed into a deeper, more potent blend of emotions.

"What are you thinking?" she asked, toying with the fringe on the wrap.

"Truthfully?"

She looked up at that, her gaze questioning. "Of course. No more secrets, remember?"

He nodded. Swallowed hard. "I'm thinking I've never felt so much at peace as I do right now."

The smile started at one corner of her lush mouth and worked its way across like the sun peeking from behind a bank of clouds. She gave him a slow, tender kiss that sizzled from his lips to the soles of his feet, before leaning back on her arms, that glorious hair a waterfall down her back.

"You know, I was never going to talk to you again

after what happened earlier. I had a relationship a while ago with a guy who lied to me. I swore then, never again." She glanced at him, then went back to staring at the sky. "God help me, I want to believe in you. I've seen the care you give to your family, the pride you take in your work, I know you're nothing like him, but..."

Anger coursed through his blood at the thought of the bastard who'd taken away her trust. If Val had been around... If he'd been around, chances were he would have still been so disillusioned by his own relationship he would've had his head in a bottle and not been any help at all.

"Guys are jerks," he agreed, his lips quirking when she looked at him, startled. "What? I can admit we spend more time thinking with our little heads than using our brains. But, and that's a big but, it's wrong to tar us all with the same brush." She stiffened and he hurried to add, "I'm just as guilty. My wife dumped me for the bright lights. Nothing I did ever seemed to please her, but I've learned something recently—it wasn't me, it was us."

He finished his wine and laid the glass on its side so it wouldn't fall. "We wanted different things, it just took us a while to figure that out."

She lifted her knees and curled her arms around them, resting her head so she could look at him with empathetic eyes that left him uncomfortable and warm at the same time. “We’re quite the pair, aren’t we?” she said. “Bruised but not broken.”

Yes, that was exactly right. “Older and wiser?” he quipped.

She lifted her head and laughed, the sound sending bubbles rushing through his blood. “Speak for yourself, mister. No woman wants her man to think of her as old.”

He smiled, and then the words sunk in.

Her man.

Her eyes grew wide, the flushed cheeks apparent even by moonlight. “A man,” she sputtered. “I meant to say… a man.”

The words died as he reached out and cupped her beloved face in his hand. “Don’t,” he murmured. “I’ve been sitting here wondering what I could do to persuade you to give me a chance and then you seemed to answer my prayers and my heart sang.” He kissed her softly parted lips. “Will you, Sierra Johnson? Will you give *this* man a chance?” He leaned his forehead against hers and waited for her answer with baited breath. They may not know each other well yet, but the connection between them was strong. He wanted the opportunity to explore where it might lead.

She sighed and wrapped her arms around his neck, creating a warm cocoon. “I thought you’d never ask,” she whispered.

Valentine's chest expanded and he blinked hard, surprised by how much her words meant to him. She'd given him a gift tonight. He swore then and there he would never take her love for granted.

He hugged her back and stared up at the house that had brought them together. Cupid sat on the deck staring at the two lovebirds, and Valentine swore he saw a smile.

CHAPTER
SEVENTEEN

O*ne year later*

Sierra hurried to place the final touches on the lavishly decorated hall. There wasn't much time until the guests arrived, and she needed everything perfect for this special day. She'd gone with a subdued blue-gray tone in deference of the groom-to-be, and then added bright pops of crimson, yellow and white for the bride. This would be the first big function since opening the doors of the Tickled Pink Designing Company and she planned to make a splash.

"Don't you think it's time for you to go and get ready?" Norma Jean asked, her blond curls bouncing as she walked across the hall in heels that defied gravity.

Valentine had been right, once Sierra got over her jealousy she'd found the other woman to be sweet, kind, and funny. They quickly became fast friends and partners in the new business—a blend of catering and planning. Seems that Norma Jean's daddy came from money—old money—and he didn't mind backing his daughter's crazy schemes.

Not that this was one of those.

Nope. Sierra had dreamed of this day her whole life, and only one thing could make it better.

"Anyone call a cab?"

She whirled around, a smile flirting with her lips even as she made shooing motions with her hands. "You promised you'd wait," she admonished her fiancé.

Valentine strolled into the room, handsome in a navy sweater and linen pants, Cupid trailing behind with his nose in the air. "I received a message my beautiful bride was working her fingers to the bone and I better hurry or there won't be a wedding night." He gave Norma Jean a conspirator's wink.

Sierra gasped in mock outrage. "I knew you two were sneaking around behind my back." She laughed and reached up to kiss her man. His unending faith, generosity, and the passion they shared had taught her love was possible—with the right person.

When his great-aunt came home from the hospital, Val had a ramp installed and hired a fulltime care worker to help out around the brownstone. His aunt had offered them a home for as long as they wanted, and it was working out well. He'd sold his condo in Vancouver and rerouted his clientele to the island where business was booming.

She gazed around the room that would be filled with their family and friends in just a few short hours. Sierra could barely believe the changes in her life. A year ago, she'd been depressed and lonely with no future in sight. She smiled up a Valentine with her heart in her eyes. She really was about to marry her prince. He'd ensured all her dreams had come true. Cupid nestled between their legs with soulful brown eyes and they started to laugh.

Life was good.

PREVIEW WITH THIS HEART

She yanked the door open and then jumped backward with a shriek as a brown and white shape hurtled through the gap and stumbled in the drive.

"Dad, save Bambi," Chris cried from inside the cab.

"What was that?" Annie whispered, hands clenched to her chest.

Jared was torn between taking her into his arms or checking on the injured animal for his son. A further cry from Chris as he scrambled to get out of the pickup cemented his decision. He sent a quick glance Annie's way before hurrying to kneel beside the fawn and stop its frantic movements. "Son, bring that blanket with you. His scent is on it now, it may reassure him some."

"Is he okay?" Chris hopped down from the crew cab, tugging the blanket behind him. "Hi, Mom," he chirped on his way by, "guess what Jared did? He hit a baby deer." The last was said with a mix of nervous tension.

Jared looked up in time to see Annie's scowl turn to concern. He held out his hand for the quilt. "Here, I'll cover him up and then you keep him still while I call the vet. Deal?"

"Deal," Chris agreed, plopping onto the grass and startling the fawn. He scrunched his shoulders and shrugged. "Sorry."

Jared smiled. "Just take it easy around him for the first few days. You have to remember he's not used to people. This is all very strange for him." He wrapped the trembling body, careful to avoid the bad leg. "Pet his head like I showed you before and I'll be right back, okay?"

Chris nodded without looking away from the delicate face of the deer. "Sure, we're friends already, see?" He proceeded to rub between the fawn's ears. "He likes me."

"Well, sure he does. What's not to like?" Jared rumpled his son's red hair—so like his mother's—and rose. After making sure the fawn was content, he turned to Annie. "Sorry we couldn't call. Reception was bad out there."

"What if you'd been injured?" Annie sniped under her breath so as not to alert Chris. "I had no idea where you'd gone. Where to search. It was an irresponsible thing to do." She folded defensive arms across her chest.

"Whoa, where is this coming from?" Jared grasped her forearm and pulled her resisting body to the front of the truck. "Sweetheart, it's not like I planned on driving home in the dark and clipping a fawn during our first father-son road trip. You're not being fair."

"Fair?" she cried. "Chris is *my* son, Jared. I have the right to know he's safe."

Stunned, he released her arm. "Actually, I thought he was *our* son. What's going on, Annie?"

She stared up at him with tear-drenched eyes. "Maybe we're a mistake." She looked at his dented vehicle, and at Chris caring for the injured deer, before meeting his gaze with a defiant lift of her chin. "I don't think I can marry you anymore."

MY GIFT TO YOU!

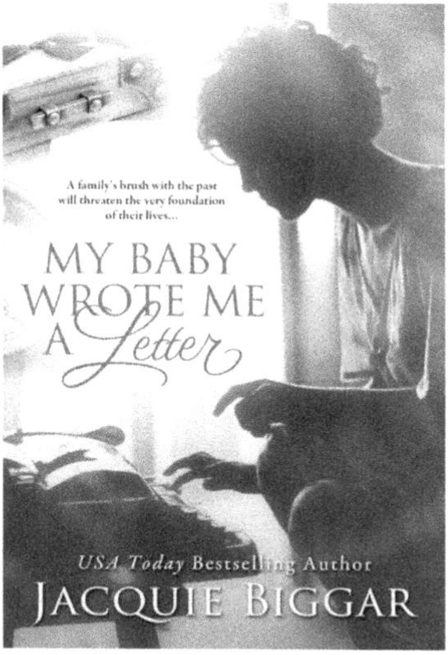

My Baby Wrote Me A Letter

A family's brush with the past will threaten the fabric of their lives.

Eight months pregnant and her Navy husband away on a mission, Grace Freeman craves the security of her childhood home in Canada.

When a letter written by her long-lost mother is found in an old writing desk it creates a tear in the fabric of her family.

Can Grace find a way to bring peace to those she loves, or will a message from the past destroy their future?

Newsletter subscribers also get bonus content and insider information every month. I love giveaways and there is lots of interesting stuff for me to share with you!

Newsletter- Sign up Now!

AFTERWORD

Reviews are the lifeblood of any successful author. Without you, we can't be heard.

If you enjoy the story, please consider sharing on your favorite social media sites, as well as GoodReads and from wherever you've bought the book.

Thank you,

Jacquie Biggar

Jacqbiggar.com

Also by Jacquie Biggar

Wounded Hearts Series

Tidal Falls

The Rebel's Redemption

Twilight's Encore

The Sheriff Meets His Match

Summer Lovin'

Wounded Hearts Box Set

Maggie's Revenge

With This Heart

The SEAL's Temptation

Secrets, Lies & Alibis

Mended Souls Series

The Guardian

The Beast Within

Virtually Gone

GAMBLING HEARTS

Hold 'Em

Crazy Little Thing Called Love

My Girl

Married to The Texan- Box set

BLUE HAVEN

Sweetheart Cove

Sunset Beach

MEN OF WARHAWKS

Skating on Thin Ice

The Player

THE DEFIANT SISTERS DUET

Letting Go

Finding Me

SINGLE TITLES

Silver Bells

The Lady Said No

My Baby Wrote Me A Letter

Tempted by Mr. Wrong

Valentine: A Hearts and Kisses Romance

Mistletoe Inn

The Sister Pact

Perfectly Imperfect

Love, Me

About the Author

JACQUIE BIGGAR is a USA Today bestselling author of Romantic Suspense who loves to write about tough, alpha males and strong, contemporary women willing to show their men that true power comes from love.

She is the author of the popular Wounded Hearts series and has just started a new series in paranormal suspense, Mended Souls.

She has been blessed with a long, happy marriage and enjoys writing romance novels that end with happily-ever-afters.

Jacquie lives in paradise along the west coast of Canada with her family and loves reading, writing, and flower gardening. She swears she can't function without coffee, preferably at the beach with her sweetheart. :)

Sign up now to keep up with Jacquie's new releases, excerpts, giveaways, and more: Newsletter

jacqbiggar.com

jbiggar@jacqbiggar.com

facebook.com/jacqbiggar

twitter.com/jacqbiggar

instagram.com/jacqbiggar

amazon.com/author/jacquiebiggar

bookbub.com/authors/jacquie-biggar

goodreads.com/JacquieBiggar

Milton Keynes UK
Ingram Content Group UK Ltd.
UKHW020644070923
428220UK00012B/354

9 798223 543404